HORRID HENRY STRIKES IT RICH

HORRID HENRY STRIKES IT RICH

Francesca Simon

Illustrated by Tony Ross

SCHOLASTIC INC.

New York Toronto London Auckland Sydney
Mexico City New Delhi Hong Kong

Horrid Henry Runs Away and *Horrid Henry Strikes it Rich* were first published in Great Britain by Orion Children's Books in 1998. *Horrid Henry's Shot* and *Perfect Peter's Horrid Day* were first published in Great Britain by Orion Chidren's Books in 1995.

ISBN 0-439-28683-2

12 11 10 9 8 7 6 5 4 3 2   1 2 3 4 5 6/0

Printed in the U.S.A.   40

First Scholastic printing, April 2001

For Joshua and his classmates in 4H,
with thanks for all their help

CONTENTS

Chapter 1

PERFECT PETER'S HORRID DAY

"Henry, use your fork!" said Dad.

"*I'm* using my fork," said Peter.

"Henry, sit down!" said Mom.

"*I'm* sitting down," said Peter.

"Henry, stop spitting!" said Dad.

"*I'm* not spitting," said Peter.

"Henry, chew with your mouth shut!" said Mom.

"*I'm* chewing with my mouth shut," said Peter.

"Henry, don't make a mess!" said Dad.

"*I'm* not making a mess," said Peter.

"What?" said Mom.

Perfect Peter was not having a perfect day.

Mom and Dad are too busy yelling at Henry all the time to notice how good *I* am, thought Peter.

When was the last time Mom and Dad had said, "Marvelous, Peter, you're using your fork!" "Wonderful, Peter, you're sitting down!" "Superb, Peter, you're not spitting!" "Fabulous, Peter, you're chewing with your mouth shut!" "Perfect, Peter, you never make a mess!"

Perfect Peter dragged himself upstairs.

Everyone just expects me to be perfect, thought Peter, as he wrote his Aunt Agnes a thank-you note for the super thermal vests. It's not fair.

From downstairs came the sound of raised voices.

"Henry, get your muddy shoes off the sofa!" yelled Dad.

"Henry, stop being so horrid!" yelled Mom.

Then Perfect Peter started to think.

What if I were horrid? thought Peter.

Peter's mouth dropped open. What a horrid thought! He looked around quickly, to see if anyone had noticed.

He was alone in his immaculate bedroom. No one would ever know he'd thought such a terrible thing.

But imagine being horrid. No, that would never do.

Peter finished his letter, read a few pages of his favorite magazine, *Best Boy*, got into bed, and turned off his light without being asked.

Imagine being horrid.

What if I were horrid, thought Peter. I wonder what would happen?

When Peter woke up the next morning, he did not dash downstairs to get breakfast ready. Instead, he lazed in bed for an extra five minutes.

When he finally got up, Peter did not make his bed.

Nor did Peter fluff his pillows.

Instead, Peter looked at his tidy bedroom and had a very wicked thought.

Quickly, before he could change his mind, he took off his pajama top and did not fold it neatly. Instead, he dropped it on the floor.

Mom came in.

"Good morning, darling. You must be tired, sleeping in."

Peter hoped Mom would notice his untidy room.

But Mom did not say anything.

"Notice anything, Mom?" said Peter.

His mother looked around.

"No," said Mom.

"Oh," said Peter.

"What?" said Mom.

"I haven't made my bed," said Peter.

"Clever of you to remember it's laundry day," said Mom. She stripped the sheets and blankets, then swooped and picked up Peter's pajama top.

"Thank you, dear," said Mom. She smiled and left.

Peter frowned. Clearly, he would need to work harder at being horrid.

He looked at his beautifully arranged books.

"No!" he gasped, as a dreadful thought sneaked into his head.

Then Peter squared his shoulders. Today was his horrid day, and horrid he would be. He went up to his books and knocked them over.

"**HENRY!**" bellowed his father. "Get up this minute!"

Henry slumped past Peter's door.

Peter decided he would call Henry a horrid name.

"Hello, Ugly," said Peter. Then he went wild and stuck out his tongue.

Henry marched into Peter's bedroom. He glared at Peter.

"What did you call me?" said Henry.

Peter screamed.

5

Mom ran into the room.

"Stop being horrid, Henry! Look what a mess you've made in here!"

"He called me Ugly," said Henry.

"Of course he didn't," said Mom.

"He did too," said Henry.

"Peter never calls people names," said Mom. "Now pick up those books you knocked over."

"I didn't knock them over," said Henry.

"Well, who did, then, the man in the moon?" said Mom.

Henry pointed at Peter.

"He did," said Henry.

"*Did* you, Peter?" asked Mom.

Peter wanted to be really really horrid and tell a lie. But he couldn't.

"I did it, Mom," said Peter. Boy, would he get told off now.

"Don't be silly, of course you didn't," said Mom. "You're just saying that to protect Henry."

Mom smiled at Peter and frowned at Henry.

"Now leave Peter alone and get dressed," said Mom.

"But it's the weekend," said Henry.

7

"So?" said Mom.

"But Peter's not dressed."

"I'm sure he was just about to get dressed before you barged in," said Mom. "See? He's already taken his pajama top off."

"I don't want to get dressed," said Peter boldly.

"You poor boy," said Mom. "You must be feeling ill. Pop back into bed and I'll bring your breakfast up. Just let me put some clean sheets on."

Perfect Peter scowled a tiny scowl. Clearly, he wasn't very good at being horrid yet. He would have to try harder.

At lunch Peter ate pasta with his fingers. No one noticed.

Then Henry scooped up pasta with both fists and slurped some into his mouth.

"Henry! Use your fork!" said Dad.

Peter spat into his plate.

"Peter, are you choking?" said Dad.

Henry spat across the table.

"Henry! Stop that disgusting spitting this instant!" said Mom.

Peter chewed with his mouth open.

"Peter, is there something wrong with your teeth?" asked Mom.

Henry chomped and dribbled and gulped with his mouth as wide open as possible.

"Henry! This is your last warning. Keep your mouth shut when you eat!" shouted Dad.

Peter did not understand. Why didn't anyone notice how horrid he was? He stretched out his foot and kicked Henry under the table.

9

Henry kicked him back harder.

Peter shrieked.

Henry got told off. Peter got dessert.

Perfect Peter did not know what to do. No matter how hard he tried to be horrid, nothing seemed to work.

"Now, boys," said Mom, "Grandma is coming for tea this afternoon. Please keep the house tidy and leave the chocolates alone."

"What chocolates?" said Henry.

"Never you mind," she said. "You'll have some when Grandma gets here."

Suddenly Peter had a truly stupendously horrid idea. He left the table without waiting to be excused and sneaked into the sitting room.

Peter searched high. Peter searched low. Then Peter found a large box of chocolates hidden behind some books.

Peter opened the box. Then he took a tiny bite out of every single chocolate. When he found good ones with gooey chocolate fudge centers he ate them. The yucky raspberry and strawberry and lemon creams he put back.

Hee hee, thought Peter. He felt excited. What he had done was absolutely awful. Mom and Dad were sure to notice.

Then Peter looked around the tidy sitting room. Why not mess it up a bit?

Peter grabbed a cushion from the sofa. He was just about to fling it on the floor when he heard someone sneaking into the room.

"What are you doing?" said Henry.

"Nothing, Ugly," said Peter.

"Don't call me Ugly, Toad," said Henry.

11

"Don't call me Toad, Ugly," said Peter.
"Toad!"
"Ugly!"
"TOAD!"
"UGLY!"
Mom and Dad ran in.
"Henry!" shouted Dad. "Stop being horrid!"

"I'm not being horrid!" said Henry. "Peter is calling me names."

Mom and Dad looked at each other. What was going on?

"Don't lie, Henry," said Mom.

"I did call him a name, Mom," said Peter. "I called him Ugly because he is ugly. So there."

Mom stared at Peter.

Dad stared at Peter.

Henry stared at Peter.

"If Peter did call you a name, it's because you called him one first," said Mom. "Now leave Peter alone."

Mom and Dad left.

"Serves you right, Henry," said Peter.

"You're very strange today," said Henry.

"No I'm not," said Peter.

"Oh yes you are," said Henry. "You can't fool me. Listen, want to play a trick on Grandma?"

"No!" said Peter.

Ding dong.

"Grandma's here!" called Dad.

Mom, Dad, Henry, Peter, and Grandma sat down together in the sitting room.

"Let me take your bag, Grandma," said Henry sweetly.

"Thank you, dear," said Grandma.

When no one was looking, Henry took

13

Grandma's glasses out of her bag and hid them behind Peter's cushion.

Mom and Dad passed around tea and home-made cookies on the best china plates.

Peter sat on the edge of the sofa and held his breath. Any second now Mom would get out the box of half-eaten chocolates.

Mom stood up and got the box.

"Peter, would you like to pass around the chocolates?" said Mom.

"Okay," said Peter. His knees felt wobbly. Everyone was about to find out what a horrid thing he had done.

Peter held out the box.

"Would you like a chocolate, Mom?" said Peter. His heart pounded.

"No thanks," said Mom.

"What about me?" said Henry.

"Would you like a chocolate, Dad?" said Peter. His hands shook.

"No thanks," said Dad.

"What about me!" said Henry.

"Shh, Henry," said Mom. "Don't be so rude."

"Would you like a chocolate, Grandma?" said Peter.

There was no escape now. Grandma loved chocolates.

"Yes, please!" said Grandma. She peered closely into the box. "Let me see, what shall I choose? Now, where are my specs?"

Grandma reached into her bag and fumbled about.

"That's funny," said Grandma. "I was sure I'd brought them. Never mind."

Grandma reached into the box, chose a chocolate, and popped it into her mouth.

"Oh," said Grandma. "Strawberry cream. Go on, Peter, have a chocolate."

"No thanks," said Peter.

"WHAT ABOUT ME!" screamed Horrid Henry.

"None for you," said Dad. "That's not how you ask."

Peter gritted his teeth. If no one was going to notice the chewed chocolates he'd have to do it himself.

15

"I will have a chocolate," announced Peter loudly. "Hey! Who's eaten all the fudge ones? And who's taken bites out of the rest?"

"Henry!" yelled Mom. "I've told you a million times to leave the chocolates alone!"

"It wasn't me!" said Henry. "It was Peter!"

"Stop blaming Peter," said Dad. "You know he never eats candy."

"It's not fair!" shrieked Henry. Then he snatched the box from Peter. "I want some CHOCOLATES!"

Peter snatched it back. The open box fell to the floor. Chocolates flew everywhere.

"HENRY, GO TO YOUR ROOM!" yelled Mom.

"IT'S NOT FAIR!" screeched Henry. *"I'll get you for this, Peter!"*

Then Horrid Henry ran out of the room, slamming the door behind him.

Grandma patted the sofa beside her. Peter sat down. He could not believe it. What did a boy have to do to get noticed?

"How's my best boy?" asked Grandma.

Peter sighed.

Grandma gave him a big hug. "You're the best boy in the world, Peter, did you know that?"

Peter glowed. Grandma was right! He was the best.

But wait. **Today he was horrid.**

NO! He was perfect. His horrid day was over.

He was much happier being perfect, anyway. Being horrid was horrible.

I've had my horrid day, thought Peter. Now I can be perfect again.

What a marvelous idea. Peter smiled and leaned back against the cushion.

CRUNCH!

17

"Oh dear," said Grandma. "That sounds like my specs. I wonder how they got there."

Mom looked at Peter.

Dad looked at Peter.

"It wasn't me!" said Peter.

"Of course not," said Grandma. "I must have dropped them. Silly me."

"Hmmm," said Dad.

Perfect Peter ran into the kitchen and looked around. Now that I'm perfect again, what good deeds can I do? he thought.

Then Peter noticed all the dirty teacups and plates piled up on the counter. He had never done the washing up all by himself before. Mom and Dad would be so pleased.

Peter carefully washed and dried all the dishes.

Then he stacked them up and carried them to the cupboard.

"*BOOOOOOO!*" shrieked Horrid Henry, leaping out from behind the door.

CRASH!

Henry vanished.

Mom and Dad ran in.

The best china lay in pieces all over the floor.

"PETER!!!" yelled Mom and Dad.

"YOU HORRID BOY!" yelled Mom.

"GO TO YOUR ROOM!" yelled Dad.

"But . . . but . . ." gasped Peter.

"NO BUTS!" shouted Mom. "GO! Oh, my lovely dishes!"

"A H H H H H H H H H H H H H ! " shrieked Peter.

Chapter 2
HORRID HENRY'S SHOT

"AAHH!!"

"AAAHHH!!!"

"AAAHHHH!!!"

"AAAAAHHHHH!!!!"

The horrible screams came from behind Nurse Needle's closed door.

Horrid Henry looked at his younger brother, Perfect Peter. Perfect Peter looked at Horrid Henry. Then they both looked at their father, who stared straight ahead.

Henry and Peter were in Dr. Dettol's waiting room.

Moody Margaret was there. So were Sour Susan, Anxious Andrew, Jolly Josh, Weepy William, Tough Toby, Lazy Linda, Clever Clare,

21

Rude Ralph, and just about everyone Henry knew. They were all waiting for the terrible moment when Nurse Needle would call their name.

Today was the worst day in the world. Today was—shot day.

Horrid Henry was not afraid of spiders.

He was not afraid of ghosts.

He was not afraid of burglars, bad dreams, squeaky doors, and things that go bump in the night. Only one thing scared him.

Just thinking about . . . about . . . Henry could barely even say the word—SHOTS—made him shiver and quiver and shake and quake.

Nurse Needle came into the waiting room.

Henry held his breath.

"Please let it be someone else," he prayed.

"William!" said Nurse Needle.

Weepy William burst into tears.

"Let's have none of that," said Nurse Needle. She took him firmly by the arm and closed the door behind him.

"I don't need a shot!" said Henry. "I feel fine."

"Shots stop you from getting ill," said Dad. "Shots fight germs."

22

"I don't believe in germs," said Henry.

"I do," said Dad.

"I do," said Peter.

"Well, I don't," said Henry.

Dad sighed. "You're getting a shot, and that's that."

"I don't mind shots," said Perfect Peter. "I know how good they are for me."

Horrid Henry pretended he was an alien who'd come from outer space to jab earthlings.

"OWW!" shrieked Peter.

"Don't be horrid, Henry!" shouted Dad.

"AAAAAAHHHHHH!" came the terrible

screams from behind Nurse Needle's door. "AAAAAAHHHHH! NOOOOOOOO!"

Then Weepy William staggered out, clutching his arm and wailing.

"Crybaby," said Henry.

"Just wait, Henry," sobbed William.

Nurse Needle came into the waiting room.

Henry closed his eyes.

Don't pick me, he begged silently. Don't pick me.

"Susan!" said Nurse Needle.

Sour Susan crept into Nurse Needle's office.

"AAAAAAHHHHHH!" came the terrible screams. "AAAAAAHHHHH! NOOOOOOO!"

Then Sour Susan dragged herself out, clutching her arm and sniveling.

"What a crybaby," said Henry.

"Well, we all know about *you*, Henry," said Susan sourly.

"Oh yeah?" said Henry. "You don't know anything."

Nurse Needle reappeared.

Henry hid his face behind his hands.

I'll be so good if it's not me, he thought. Please, let it be someone else.

24

"Margaret!" said Nurse Needle.

Henry relaxed.

"Hey, Margaret, did you know the needles are so big and sharp they can go right through your arm?" said Henry.

Moody Margaret ignored him and marched into Nurse Needle's office.

Henry could hardly wait for her terrible screams. **Boy, would he tease that crybaby Margaret!**

Silence.

Then Moody Margaret swaggered into the waiting room, proudly displaying an enormous Band-Aid on her arm. She smiled at Henry.

25

"Ooh, Henry, you won't believe the needle she's using today," said Margaret. "It's as long as my leg."

"Shut up, Margaret," said Henry. He was breathing very fast and felt faint.

"Anything wrong, Henry?" asked Margaret sweetly.

"No," said Henry. He scowled at her. How dare she not scream and cry?

"Oh, good," said Margaret. "I just wanted to warn you because I've never seen such big fat whopping needles in all my life!"

Horrid Henry steadied himself. Today would be different.

He would be brave.

He would be fearless.

He would march into Nurse Needle's office, offer his arm, and dare her to do her worst. Yes, today was the day. Brave Henry, he would be called, the boy who laughed when the needle went in, the boy who asked for a second shot, the boy who—

"Henry!" said Nurse Needle.

"NO!" shrieked Henry. "Please, please, NO!"

"Yes," said Nurse Needle. "It's your turn now."

Henry forgot he was brave.

Henry forgot he was fearless.

Henry forgot everyone was watching him.

Henry started screaming and screeching and kicking.

"OW!" yelped Dad.

"OW!" yelped Perfect Peter.

"OW!" yelped Lazy Linda.

Then everyone started screaming and screeching.

"I don't want a shot!" shrieked Horrid Henry.

"I don't want a shot!" shrieked Anxious Andrew.

"I don't want a shot!" shrieked Tough Toby.

"Stop it," said Nurse Needle. "You need a shot and a shot is what you will get."

"Him first!" screamed Henry, pointing at Peter.

"You're such a baby, Henry," said Clever Clare.

That did it.

No one *ever* called Henry a baby and lived.

He kicked Clare as hard as he could. Clare screamed.

Nurse Needle and Dad each grabbed one of Henry's arms and dragged him howling into her office. Peter followed behind, whistling softly.

Henry wriggled free and dashed out. Dad nabbed him and brought him back. Nurse Needle's door clanged shut behind them.

Henry stood in the corner. He was trapped.

Nurse Needle kept her distance. Nurse Needle knew Henry. Last time he'd had a shot he'd kicked her.

29

Dr. Dettol came in.

"What's the trouble, Nurse?" she asked.

"Him," said Nurse Needle. "He doesn't want a shot."

Dr. Dettol kept her distance. Dr. Dettol knew Henry. Last time he'd had a shot he'd bitten her.

"Take a seat, Henry," said Dr. Dettol.

Henry collapsed in a chair. There was no escape.

"What a fuss over a little thing like a shot," said Dr. Dettol. "Call me if you need me," she added, and left the room.

Henry sat on the chair, breathing hard. He tried not to look as Nurse Needle examined her gigantic pile of needles.

But he could not stop himself peeking through his fingers. He watched as she got the shot ready, choosing the longest, sharpest, most wicked needle Henry had ever seen.

Then Nurse Needle approached, weapon in hand.

"Him first!" shrieked Henry.

Perfect Peter sat down and rolled up his sleeve.

"I'll go first," said Peter. "I don't mind."

"Oh," he said, as the needle pricked his arm.

"That was perfect," said Nurse Needle.

"What a good boy you are," said Dad.

Perfect Peter smiled proudly.

Nurse Needle rearmed herself.

Horrid Henry shrank back in the chair. He looked around wildly.

Then Henry noticed the row of little medicine bottles lined up on the counter. Nurse Needle was filling her shots from them.

Henry looked closer. The labels read: "DO NOT GIVE SHOT IF A CHILD IS FEVERISH OR SEEMS ILL."

Nurse Needle came closer, brandishing the shot. Henry coughed.

And closer. Henry sneezed.

And closer. Henry wheezed and rasped and panted.

Nurse Needle lowered her arm.

"Are you all right, Henry?"

"No," gasped Henry. "I'm ill. My chest hurts, my head hurts, my throat hurts."

Nurse Needle felt his sweaty forehead.

Henry coughed again, a hacking throaty cough.

"I can't breathe," he choked. "Asthma."

"You don't have asthma, Henry," said Dad.

"I do too," said Henry, gasping for breath.

Nurse Needle frowned.

"He is a little warm," she said.

32

"I'm ill," whispered Henry pathetically. "I feel terrible."

Nurse Needle put down her needle.

"I think you'd better bring him back when he's feeling better," she said.

"All right," said Dad. He'd make sure Henry's mother brought him next time.

Henry wheezed and sneezed, moaned and groaned, all the way home. His parents put him straight to bed.

"Oh, Mom," said Henry, trying to sound as weak as possible. "Could you bring me some chocolate ice cream to soothe my throat? It really hurts."

"Of course," said Mom. "You poor boy."

Henry snuggled down in the cool sheets. Ahh, this was the life.

"Oh, Mom," added Henry, coughing. "Could you bring up the TV? Just in case my head stops hurting long enough for me to watch?"

"Of course," said Mom.

Boy, this was great! thought Henry. **No shot! No school tomorrow! Dinner in bed!**

There was a knock on the door. It must be

Mom with his ice cream. Henry sat up in bed,
then remembered he was ill. He lay back and
closed his eyes.

"Come in, Mom," said Henry hoarsely.

"Hello, Henry."

Henry opened his eyes. It wasn't Mom. **It was Dr. Dettol.**

Henry closed his eyes and had a terrible coughing fit.

"What hurts?" said Dr. Dettol.

"Everything," said Henry. "My head, my throat, my chest, my eyes, my ears, my back, and my legs."

"Oh dear," said Dr. Dettol.

She took out her stethoscope and listened to Henry's chest. All clear.

She stuck a little stick in his mouth and told him to say "AAAAAH." All clear.

She examined his eyes and his ears, his back and his legs. Everything seemed fine.

"Well, Doctor?" said Mom.

Dr. Dettol shook her head. She looked grave.

"He's very ill," said Dr Dettol. "There's only one cure."

"What?" said Mom.

"What?" said Dad.

"A shot!"

Chapter 3

HORRID HENRY RUNS AWAY

Horrid Henry was not having a good day. His younger brother, Perfect Peter, had grabbed the hammock first and wouldn't get out. Then Mom had ordered him to tidy his room just when he was watching *Rapper Zapper* on TV. And now Dad was yelling at him.

"What's the meaning of this letter, Henry?" shouted Dad.

"What letter?" snapped Henry. He was sick and tired of being nagged at.

"You know perfectly well what letter!" said Mom. "The letter from Miss Battle-Axe. The third this week."

Oh, *that* letter.

Dear Henry's Parents,

I am sorry to tell you that today Henry:
Poked William
Tripped Linda
Shoved Dave
Pinched Andrew
Made rude noises, chewed gum, and
would not stop talking in class.

Yours sincerely,
Boudicca Battle-Axe

Henry scowled.

"Can I help it if I have to burp?"

"And what about all the children you hurt?" said Dad.

"I hardly touched William. Linda got in my way, and Dave and Andrew annoyed me," said Henry. What a big fuss over nothing.

"Right," said Dad. "I am very disappointed with you. No TV, no comics, and no sweets for a week."

"A WEEK!" screamed Henry. "For giving someone a little tap? It's not fair!"

38

"What about *my* letter?" said Peter.

Dear Peter's Parents,

I am delighted to tell you that today Peter:
Helped Gordon
Shared with Sam
Volunteered to clean the paintbrushes
Picked up the balls in P.E.
Cleaned the classroom without being asked.
Well done, Peter!
He is in the Good as Gold Book for the third time this month—a school record.

Yours sincerely,
Lydia Lovely

Dad glowed. "At least *one* child in this family knows how to behave."

Peter smiled modestly.

"You really should think more about other people, Henry," said Peter. "Then maybe one day *you'll* be in the Good as Gold Book."

Horrid Henry snarled and leaped on Peter. He was primordial slime oozing over a trapped insect.

39

*"**Yeowww!**"* howled Peter.

"Stop it, Henry!" shouted Mom. "Go straight to your room. NOW!"

Horrid Henry stomped upstairs to his bedroom and slammed the door.

"That's it!" screamed Henry. "No one in this family likes me, so I'm leaving!"

He'd show his horrible parents. He would run away to the jungle. He would fight giant snakes, crush crocodiles, and paddle alone up piranha-infested rivers, hacking his way through the vines. And he'd never ever come back. Then they'd be sorry. Serve them right for being so mean to him.

He could see them now. If only we'd been

nicer to Henry, Dad would cry. Yes, such a lovely boy, Mom would sob. Why oh why were we so cruel to him? If only Henry would come home he could always have the hammock, Peter would whimper. Why was I so selfish?

A shame, really, thought Henry, dragging his suitcase from under the bed, that I won't be here to see them all wailing and gnashing their teeth.

Right, he thought, I'll only pack things I absolutely need. "Lean and mean" was the motto of Heroic Henry, Jungle Explorer.

Henry surveyed his room. What couldn't he live without?

He couldn't leave his Grisly Grub box and Dungeon Drink kit. Into the bag went the box and the kit. His Super Soaker 2000 water blaster would definitely come in handy in the wilds. And of course, lots of games in case he got bored fighting panthers.

Comics? Henry considered . . . definitely. He stuffed a big stack in his bag. A few packets of chips and some candy would be good. And the box of Day-Glo slime. Henry certainly didn't want Peter getting his sticky fingers on his precious slime. Teddy? Nah! Teddy wouldn't be any use where he was going.

Perfect, thought Henry. Then he closed the bulging case. It would not shut. Very reluctantly Henry took out one comic and his soccer ball. There, he thought. He'd be off at dawn. And wouldn't they be sorry.

Tweet tweet.

Heroic Henry, Jungle Explorer, opened his eyes and leaped out of bed. The early birds were

42

chirping. It was time to go. He flung on his jungle gear, then sneaked into Peter's room. He crept over to Peter's bed and pinched him.

"Wha—," muttered Peter.

"Shut up and listen," whispered Henry fiercely. "I'm running away from home. If you tell anyone I've gone you'll be really sorry. In fact, you'll be dead."

"I won't tell," squeaked Peter.

"Good," said Henry. "And don't you dare touch anything in my room, either."

Horrid Henry crept down the stairs.

BANG! BUMP! BANG! BUMP!

His suitcase clunked behind him. Henry froze. But no sound came from Mom and Dad's room.

At last Henry was safely down the stairs. Quietly he opened the back door and slipped into the misty garden.

He was outside. He was free! Good-bye, civilization, thought Henry. Soon he'd be steaming down the Congo in search of adventure.

Of course I'll need a new name, thought Henry, as he began his long trek. To stop Mom and Dad from tracking me down. Henry Intrepid

sounded good. Piranha Pirate also had a nice ring. And I'll need to disguise myself, too, thought Henry. He'd wait until he got to the jungle for that. He stole a quick glance behind him. No search party was after him so far.

Henry walked, and walked, and walked. His suitcase got heavier, and heavier, and heavier.

Phew! Henry was getting a bit tired dragging that case.

I feel like I've been traveling for miles, thought Henry. I think I'll stop and have a little rest at the secret hideaway. No one will find me there.

Horrid Henry clambered into the tree house and stepped on something squishy.

"AHHH!" screamed Henry.

"AHHH!" screamed the Squishy Thing.

"What are *you* doing here?" snapped Horrid Henry.

"What are *you* doing here?" snapped Moody Margaret.

"I've run away from home, if you must know," said Henry.

"So have I, and this is *my* tree house," said Margaret. "Go away."

"I can sit here if I want to," said Henry, sitting down on Margaret's sleeping bag.

"Ouch! Get off my leg," said Margaret, pushing him off.

"And don't think for a minute I'll let you come with me," said Henry.

"You can't come with me, either," said Margaret. "So where are *you* going?"

"The Congo," said Henry. He didn't know for sure exactly where that was, but he'd find it.

"Yuck," said Margaret. "Who'd want to go *there*? I'm going somewhere *much* better."

"Where, smarty-pants?" asked Henry. He eyed Margaret's rather plentiful stash of cookies.

"Susan's house," said Margaret.

Henry snorted.

"Susan's house? That's not running away."

"It is too," said Margaret.

"Isn't."

"Is."

"Isn't."

"Is. And I slept here all night," said Margaret. "Where did *you* sleep?"

Henry eyed the distance between himself and Margaret's cookies. Whistling nonchalantly, Henry stared in the opposite direction. Then, quick as a flash—*SNATCH!*

Henry grabbed a handful of cookies and stuffed them in his mouth.

"Hey, that's my running-away food!" said Margaret.

"Not anymore," said Henry, snickering.

"Right," said Margaret. She grabbed his case and opened it. Then she hooted with laughter.

"That's all the food you brought?" she sneered. "I'd like to see you get to the jungle with that. And all those comics! I bet you didn't even bring a map."

"Oh yeah," said Henry. "What did you bring?"

Margaret opened her suitcases. Henry snorted with laughter.

"Clothes! I don't need clothes in the jungle. And anyway, *I* thought of running away first," jeered Henry.

"Didn't," said Margaret.

"Did," said Henry.

"I'm going to tell your mother where you are," said Margaret, "and then you'll be in big trouble."

"If you dare," said Henry, "I'll . . . I'll go straight over and tell yours. And I'll tell her you slept here last night. Won't you be in trouble then? In fact I'll go and tell her right now."

"I'll tell yours first," said Margaret.

They stood up, glaring at each other.

A faint, familiar smell drifted into the tree house. It smelled like someone cooking.

Henry sniffed.

"What's that smell?"

Margaret sniffed.

"Pancakes," she said.

Pancakes! Only Henry's favorite breakfast.

"Whose house?"

Margaret sniffed again.

"Yours," she said sadly.

Yummy! Dad usually only made pancakes on special occasions. What could be happening? Then Henry had a terrible thought. Could it be **they were *celebrating* his departure?**

49

How dare they? Well, he'd soon put a stop to that.

Henry clambered out of the tree house and ran home.

"Mom! Dad! I'm back!" he shouted. "Where are my pancakes?"

"They're all gone," said Mom.

All gone!

"Why didn't you call me?" said Henry. "You know I love pancakes."

"We did call you," said Mom, "but you didn't come down. We thought you didn't want any."

"But I wasn't here," wailed Henry. He glared at Peter. Perfect Peter went on eating his pancakes a little faster, his arm protecting his plate.

"Peter knew I wasn't here," said Henry. Then he lunged for Peter's plate. Peter screamed and held on tight.

"Henry said he'd kill me if I told, so I didn't," shrieked Peter.

"Henry, let go of that plate and don't be so horrid to your brother!" said Dad.

Henry let go. There was only half a pancake left anyway and it had Peter's yucky germs all over it.

Dad sighed.

"All right, I'll make another batch," he said, getting up.

Henry was very surprised.

"Thanks, Dad," said Henry. He sat down at the table.

A big steaming stack of pancakes arrived. Henry poured heaps of maple syrup on top, then stuffed a huge forkful of buttery pancakes into his mouth.

Yummy!

He'd head for the Congo tomorrow.

Chapter 4

HORRID HENRY STRIKES IT RICH

Horrid Henry loved money. He loved counting money. He loved holding money. He loved spending money. There was only one problem. Horrid Henry never had any money.

He sat on his bedroom floor and rattled his empty skeleton bank. How his mean parents expected him to get by on two dollars a week pocket money he would never know. It was so unfair! Why should they have all the money when there were so many things *he* needed? Comic books. Whopper chocolate bars. A new football. More knights for his castle. Horrid Henry looked around his room, scowling. True, his shelves were filled with toys, but nothing he still wanted to play with.

"MOM!" screamed Henry.

"Stop shouting, Henry," shouted Mom. "If you have something to say, come downstairs and say it."

"I need more pocket money," said Henry. "Ralph gets five dollars a week."

"Different children get different amounts," said Mom. "I think two dollars a week is perfectly adequate."

"Well, I don't," said Henry.

"I'm very happy with my pocket money, Mom," said Perfect Peter. "I always save lots from my dollar. After all, if you look after the pennies the dollars will look after themselves."

"Quite right, Peter," said Mom, smiling.

Henry walked slowly past Peter. When Mom wasn't looking he reached out and grabbed him. He was a giant crab crushing a prawn in its claws.

"OWWW!" wailed Peter. "Henry pinched me!"

"I did not," said Henry.

54

"No pocket money for a week, Henry," said Mom.

"That's not fair!" howled Henry. "I need money!"

"You'll just have to save more," said Mom.

"No!" shouted Henry. He hated saving money.

"Then you'll have to find a way to earn some," said Mom.

Earn? Earn money? Suddenly Henry had a brilliant, fantastic idea.

"Mom, can I set up a stand and sell some stuff I don't want?"

"Like what?" said Mom.

"You know, old toys, comics, games, things I don't use anymore," said Henry.

Mom hesitated for a moment. She couldn't think of anything wrong with selling off old junk.

"All right," said Mom.

"Can I help, Henry?" said Peter.

"No way," said Henry.

"Oh, *please*," said Peter.

"Stop being horrid, Henry, and let Peter help you," said Mom, "or no stand."

"Okay," said Henry, scowling, "you can make the For Sale signs."

Horrid Henry ran to his bedroom and piled his unwanted junk into a box. He cleared his shelves of books, his wardrobe of nice clothes, and his toy box of puzzles with pieces missing.

Then Horrid Henry paused. To make big money he definitely needed a few more valuable items. Now, where could he find some?

Henry crept into Peter's room. He could sell Peter's stamp collection, or his nature kit. Nah, thought Henry, no one would want that boring stuff.

Then Henry glanced inside Mom and Dad's room. It was packed with rich pickings. Henry sauntered over to Mom's dressing table. Look at all that perfume, thought Henry, she wouldn't miss one bottle. He chose a large crystal bottle

with a swan-shaped stopper and packed it in the box. Now, what other junk could he find?

Aha! There was Dad's tennis racket. Dad never played tennis. That racket was just lying there collecting dust when it could go to a much better home.

Perfect, thought Henry, adding the racket to his collection. Then he staggered out to the pavement to set up the display.

Horrid Henry surveyed his stand. It was piled high with great bargains. He should make a fortune.

"But, Henry," said Peter, looking up from drawing a sign, "that's Dad's tennis racket. Are you sure he wants you to sell it?"

"Of course I'm sure, stupid," snapped Henry. If only he could get rid of his horrible brother wouldn't life be perfect.

Then Horrid Henry looked at Peter. What was it the Romans did with their leftover captives? **Hmm . . .** he thought. He looked again. **Hmmm . . .** he thought again.

"Peter," said Henry sweetly, "how would you like to earn some money?"

"Oh yes!" said Peter. "How?"

"We could sell you as a slave."

Perfect Peter thought for a moment.

"How much would I get?"

"Fifty cents," said Henry. "Wow," said Peter. "That means I'll have ten dollars in my piggy bank. Can I wear a For Sale sign?"

"Certainly," said Horrid Henry. He scribbled: FOR SALE $10, then placed the sign around Peter's neck.

"Now, look sharp," said Henry. "I see some customers coming."

"What's going on?" said Moody Margaret.

"Yeah, Henry, what are you doing?" said Sour Susan.

"I'm having a yard sale," said Henry. "Lots of bargains. All the money raised will go to a very good cause."

"What's that?" said Susan.

"Children in Need," said Henry. I am a child and I'm certainly in need, so that's true, he thought.

Moody Margaret picked up a punctured football.

"Bargain? This is just a lot of old junk."

59

"No it isn't," said Henry. **"Look. Puzzles, books, perfume, stuffed toys,** *and* **a slave."**

Moody Margaret looked up.

"I could use a good slave," said Margaret. "I'll give you a dollar for him."

"A dollar for an excellent slave? He's worth at least five dollars."

"Make a muscle, slave," said Moody Margaret.

Perfect Peter made a muscle.

"Hmmm," said Margaret. "Two dollars is my final offer."

"Done," said Horrid Henry. Why had he never thought of selling Peter before?

"How come I only get fifty cents when I cost two dollars?" said Peter.

"Shopkeeper's expenses," said Henry. "Now, run along with your new owner."

Business was brisk.

Rude Ralph bought some football cards.

Sour Susan bought Best Bear and Mom's perfume.

Beefy Bert bought a racing car with three wheels.

Then Aerobic Al jogged by.

"Cool racket," he said, picking up Dad's racket and giving it a few swings. "How much?"

"Twenty dollars," said Henry.

"I'll give you five," said Al.

Five dollars! That was more money than Horrid Henry got in two weeks! He was going to be rich!

"Done," said Henry.

Horrid Henry sat in the sitting room gazing happily at his stacks of money. Ten dollars! Boy, would that buy a lot of chocolate! Mom came into the room.

"Henry, have you seen my new perfume? You know, the one with the swan on top."

"No," said Henry. Yikes, he never thought she would notice.

"And where's Peter?" said Mom. "I thought he was playing with you."

"He's gone," said Henry.

Mom stared at him.

"What do you mean, gone?"

"Gone," said Henry, popping a chip into his mouth. **"I sold him."**

"You did what?" whispered Mom. Her face was pale.

"You said I could sell anything I didn't want, and I certainly didn't want Peter, so I sold him to Margaret."

Mom's jaw dropped.

"You go straight over to Margaret's and buy him back!" screamed Mom. "You horrid boy! Selling your own brother!"

"But I don't want him back," said Henry.

"No ifs or buts, Henry!" screeched Mom. "You just get your brother back."

"I can't afford to buy him," said Horrid Henry. "If you want him back, you should pay for him."

"HENRY!" bellowed Mom.

"All right," grumbled Henry, getting to his feet. He sighed. What a waste of good money, he thought, climbing over the wall into Margaret's garden.

Margaret was lying by the paddling pool.

"SLAVE!" she ordered. "I'm hot! Fan me!"

Perfect Peter came out of her house carrying a large fan.

He started to wave it in Moody Margaret's direction.

"Faster, slave!" said Margaret.

Peter fanned faster.

"Slower, slave!" said Margaret.

Peter fanned slower.

"Slave! A cool drink, and make it snappy!" ordered Margaret.

Horrid Henry followed Peter back into the kitchen.

"Henry!" squeaked Peter. "Have you come to rescue me?"

"No," said Henry.

"Please!" said Peter. "I'll do anything. You can have the fifty cents."

The cash register in Henry's head started to whirl.

"Not enough," said Henry.

"I'll give you a dollar. I'll give you two dollars. I'll give you three dollars," said Peter. "She's horrible. She's even worse than you."

"Right, you can stay here forever," said Henry.

"Sorry, Henry," said Perfect Peter. "You're the best brother in the world. I'll give you all my money."

Horrid Henry looked as if he were considering this offer.

"All right, wait here," said Henry. "I'll see what I can do."

"Thank you, Henry," said Peter.

Horrid Henry went back into the garden.

"Where's my drink?" said Margaret.

"My mom says I have to have Peter back," said Henry.

Moody Margaret gazed at him.

"Oh yeah?"

"Yeah," said Henry.

"Well, I don't want to sell him," said Margaret. "I paid good money for him."

Henry had hoped she'd forgotten that.

"Okay, here's the two dollars," he said.

Moody Margaret lay back and closed her eyes.

"I haven't spent all this time and effort training him just to get my money back," she said. "He's worth at least twenty dollars now."

Slowly Henry stuck his hand back into his pocket.

"Five dollars and that's my final offer."

Moody Margaret knew a good deal when she was offered one.

"Okay," she said. "Give me my money."

Reluctantly, Henry paid her. But that still leaves eight dollars, thought Henry, so I'm well ahead.

Then he went in to fetch Peter.

"You cost me ten dollars," he said.

"Thank you, Henry," said Peter. "I'll pay you as soon as we get home."

Yippee! thought Horrid Henry. I'm super-rich! The world is mine!

Clink, clank, clink, went Henry's heavy pockets as Henry did his money dance:

"I'm rich, I'm rich, I'm rich,
I'm rich as I can be," sang Henry.

"Spend, spend, spend" would be his motto from now on.

"Hello, everybody," called Dad, coming through the front door. "What a lovely afternoon! Anyone for tennis?"

Francesca Simon has written a number of funny books for children, including *Horrid Henry, Calling All Toddlers,* and *Camels Don't Ski*.

She lives in England with her husband and son.

Tony Ross's clever illustrations have added an extra laugh to many children's books, most notably the Amber Brown series by Paula Danziger.

He also lives in England.